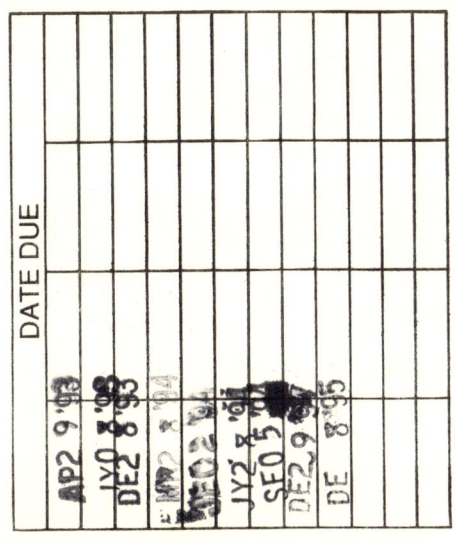

```
R584246
   12.96
E
Sch
Schulz
Talk is cheep, Charlie Brown
```

DATE DUE

GREAT RIVER REGIONAL LIBRARY
St. Cloud, Minnesota 56301

TALK IS CHEEP, CHARLIE BROWN

Charles M. Schulz

TOPPER BOOKS
AN IMPRINT OF PHAROS BOOKS • A SCRIPPS HOWARD COMPANY
NEW YORK

Copyright © 1988 United Feature Syndicate, Inc.
All rights reserved. No part of this book may be
reproduced in any form or by any means
without permission of the publisher.

PEANUTS Comic Strips: © 1986
United Feature Syndicate, Inc.

Library of Congress Catalog Card Number: 88-60377
Pharos ISBN: 0-88687-379-7

An Imprint of Pharos Books
A Scripps Howard Company
200 park Avenue
New York, NY 10166

10 9 8 7 6 5 4 3 2

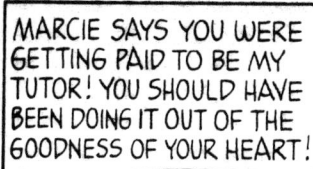

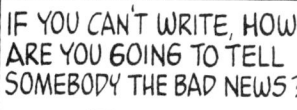

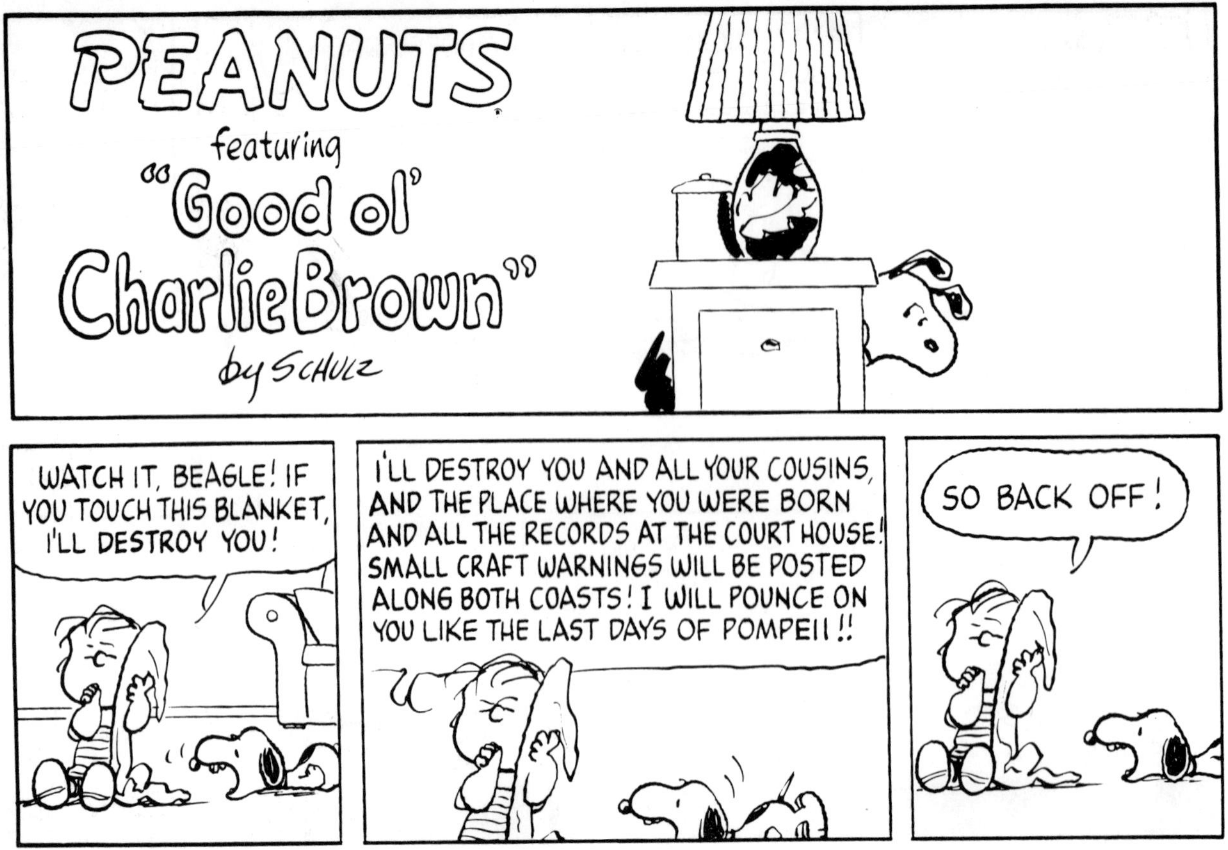

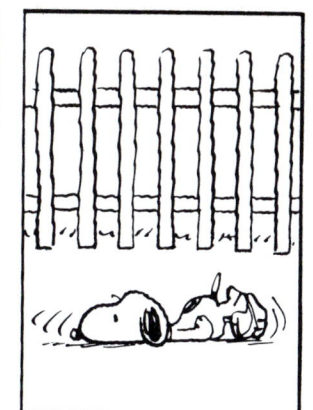

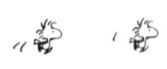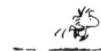

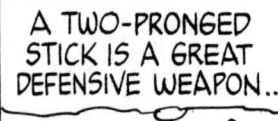

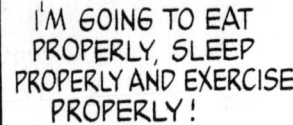

THE TEACHER WANTS US TO DO WHAT?
© 1986 United Feature Syndicate, Inc.
WALK UP TO THE FRONT OF THE ROOM, AND INTRODUCE OURSELVES.. WE ALWAYS DO IT ON THE FIRST DAY OF SCHOOL...
9-2
IT'S TOO FAR..
TOO FAR?
IT'S THIRTY MILES FROM MY DESK TO THE FRONT OF THE ROOM
SCHULZ

ME? MY TURN? YES, MA'AM
© 1986 United Feature Syndicate, Inc.
MY NAME IS CHARLES BROWN..MY DAD IS A BARBER...I GUESS MY FAVORITE HOBBIES ARE BASEBALL AND READING
I THOUGHT I DID PRETTY GOOD..WHY DID EVERYONE LAUGH?
9-3
YOU WALKED OUT THE DOOR, AND GAVE YOUR SPEECH IN THE HALLWAY!
SCHULZ

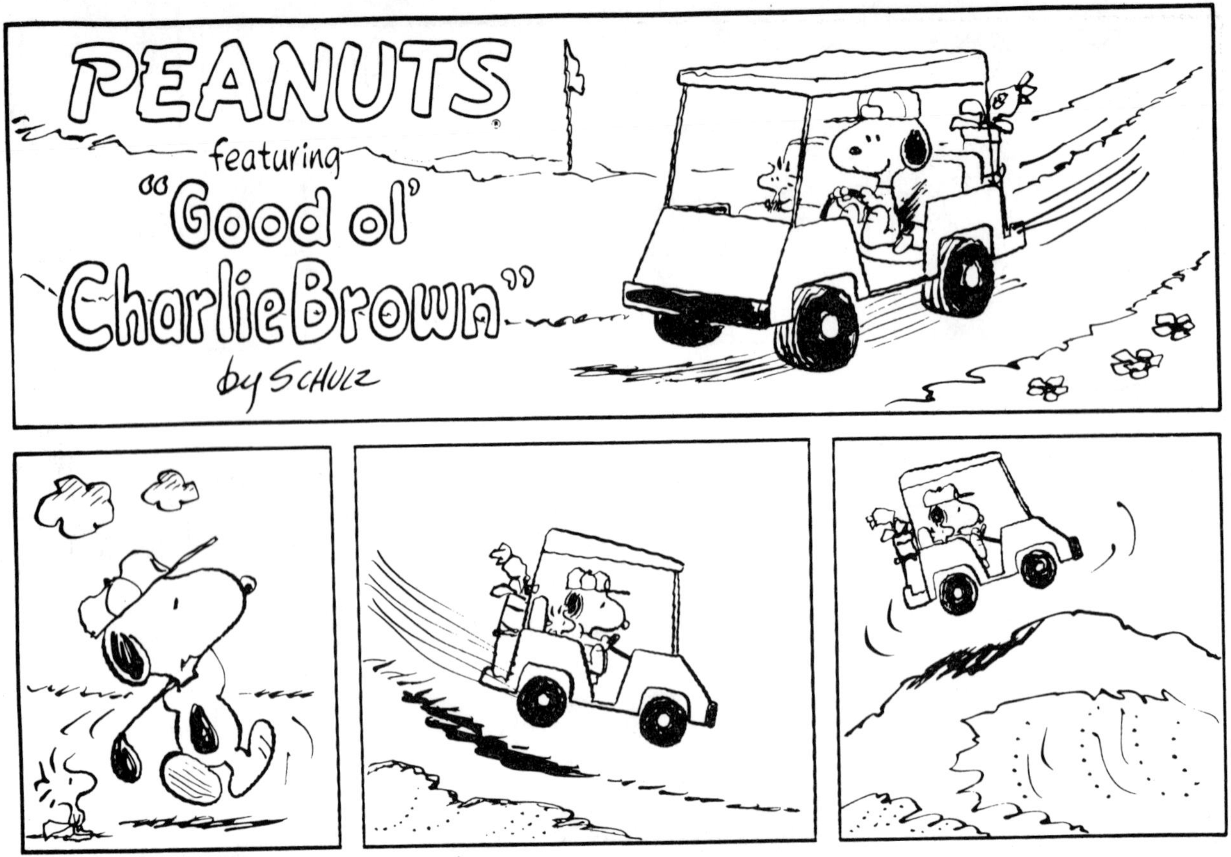
PEANUTS
featuring
"Good ol' Charlie Brown"
by SCHULZ

© 1986 United Feature Syndicate, Inc.
8-17
REMEMBER WHERE THE PRO SHOP IS? OKAY, RUN BACK THERE...
HERE'S WHAT I WANT YOU TO TELL THEM..
SCHULZ

GOOD MORNING..I'M NEW HERE IN THIS SCHOOL..I SHALL NOW INTRODUCE MYSELF...
MY NAME IS TAPIOCA PUDDING
WITH MY NAME, MY BLOND HAIR AND MY SMILE, MY DAD SAYS WE CAN MAKE A MILLION DOLLARS..
9-4
© 1986 United Feature Syndicate,Inc.
MY DAD IS IN LICENSING!
SCHULZ

EXCUSE ME..WHAT DID YOU SAY YOUR NAME IS?
TAPIOCA PUDDING... MY DAD GAVE ME MY NAME.. HE'S IN LICENSING...
9-5
© 1986 United Feature Syndicate,Inc.
HE SAID I'M GOING TO BE ON GREETING CARDS, LUNCH BOXES, TV AND EVERYTHING!
BUT, OBVIOUSLY, NO BEER COMMERCIALS..
OBVIOUSLY
SCHULZ

HI! MY NAME IS TAPIOCA PUDDING!
SOMEDAY WOULDN'T YOU LIKE TO OWN A LUNCH BOX OR A T-SHIRT WITH MY PICTURE ON IT?
© 1986 United Feature Syndicate,Inc.
LICENSING IS VERY BIG THESE DAYS!
SCHULZ
9-6

HI, MY NAME IS TAPIOCA PUDDING!
I KNOW.. MAY I SIT WITH YOU?
MY DAD DOESN'T WANT ME TO THINK ABOUT MARRIAGE YET..
WHO SAID ANYTHING ABOUT MARRIAGE?
WE'RE GOING TO HIT IT BIG IN LICENSING... MY PICTURE WILL BE ON T-SHIRTS AND EVERYTHING!
9-8
SCHULZ
WOULDN'T YOU BUY A T-SHIRT WITH MY PICTURE ON IT?
I CAN'T STAND IT..
© 1986 United Feature Syndicate,Inc.

YOU SEE, MY DAD'S NAME IS JOE PUDDING SO IT WAS ONLY NATURAL THAT I'D BE CALLED TAPIOCA PUDDING..
MY DAD'S IN LICENSING, YOU KNOW
I KNOW
© 1986 United Feature Syndicate, Inc.
WITH MY NAME AND FACE ON EVERY GREETING CARD AND CEREAL BOX IN THE COUNTRY, MY DAD SAYS WE'LL MAKE A MILLION..
9-9
YOU DON'T KNOW ANYTHING ABOUT INVESTMENTS, DO YOU?
SCHULZ

HI, MY NAME IS TAPIOCA PUDDING!
I KNOW
YOU WOULDN'T CARE TO GO TO THE MOVIES WITH ME, WOULD YOU?
9-10
AFTERWARDS, WE COULD STOP AND GET SOME ICE CREAM..
© 1986 United Feature Syndicate, Inc.
I'D RATHER JUST HAVE ROYALTY PAYMENTS..
SCHULZ

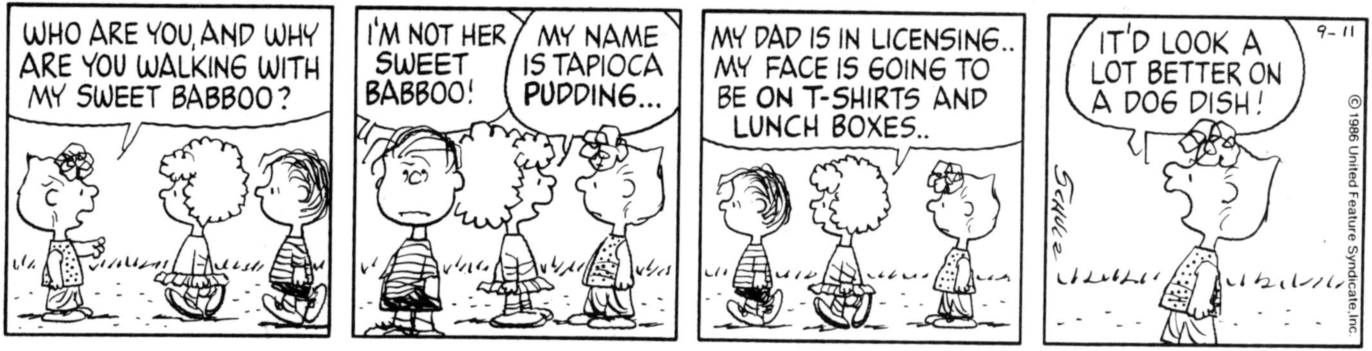
WHO ARE YOU, AND WHY ARE YOU WALKING WITH MY SWEET BABBOO?
I'M NOT HER SWEET BABBOO!
MY NAME IS TAPIOCA PUDDING...
MY DAD IS IN LICENSING.. MY FACE IS GOING TO BE ON T-SHIRTS AND LUNCH BOXES..
IT'D LOOK A LOT BETTER ON A DOG DISH!
9-11
SCHULZ
© 1986 United Feature Syndicate, Inc.

I CAN'T BELIEVE IT! I JUST SAW LINUS WALKING ALONG WITH THAT GRAPE JELLY PERSON!
HER NAME IS TAPIOCA PUDDING
9-12
© 1986 United Feature Syndicate, Inc.
TAPIOCA PUDDING! BLUEBERRY MUFFIN! WHAT'S SHE DOING WITH MY BOY FRIEND?!
I DIDN'T KNOW YOU WERE THE JEALOUS TYPE...
I KEEP IT ALL INSIDE!!
SCHULZ

THAT WAS A GOOD MOVIE..REBECCA'S MY FAVORITE ACTRESS..
9-13
I WONDER IF SHE'S INTO LICENSING... DID I TELL YOU THAT'S WHAT I'M GOING TO DO?
MY NAME WILL BE ON EVERY PRODUCT IN THE COUNTRY, AND.......... AM I BORING YOU?
© 1986 United Feature Syndicate, Inc.
NO, I ALWAYS LIKE TO REST MY FACE IN A MARSHMALLOW SUNDAE!
SCHULZ

I'M SO EXCITED! I THINK I'VE FOUND AN AGENT!
I'M MEETING HIM RIGHT AFTER SCHOOL TODAY.. HERE'S THE CARD HE SENT ME...
© 1986 United Feature Syndicate, Inc.
9-15
" ACE LICENSING." SOUNDS IMPRESSIVE...
HERE'S THE WORLD FAMOUS AGENT ON HIS WAY TO SIGN UP ANOTHER CLIENT..
SCHULZ

YOU'RE MY AGENT? I WAS EXPECTING SOMEONE SORT OF TALLER..
YOU GOT ME A JOB? THAT'S WONDERFUL!
A PERSONAL APPEARANCE, HUH? WOW!!
9-16
"OPENING CEREMONIES AT THE OLYMPIC GAMES IN LOS ANGELES"
© 1986 United Feature Syndicate, Inc.

MY AGENT JUST GOT ME A PERSONAL APPEARANCE AT THE OPENING CEREMONIES OF THE OLYMPIC GAMES IN LOS ANGELES!
THE OLYMPIC GAMES WERE TWO YEARS AGO
WHERE'S THAT AGENT? I'LL POUND HIM!!
9-17
© 1986 United Feature Syndicate, Inc.
WE'D BETTER SAY GOODBYE, SWEETIE.. I LEAVE FOR FRANCE AT MIDNIGHT...
SCHULZ

PEANUTS
featuring "Good ol' Charlie Brown"
by SCHULZ
YES, SIR..I NEED SOME SCHOOL SUPPLIES..
© 1986 United Feature Syndicate, Inc.
I NEED A LOOSE-LEAF BINDER, SOME PAPER, A RULER, SIX PENCILS AND A BALL POINT PEN..

MARCIE! JUST THE PERSON I WANTED TO SEE!
I NEED TO BORROW SOME SCHOOL SUPPLIES..I NEED A LOOSE-LEAF BINDER, SOME PAPER, A RULER, SIX PENCILS AND A BALL POINT PEN..
9-7
THANKS, MARCIE..I REALLY APPRECIATE THIS...
IT'S GOING TO SEEM STRANGE BEING BACK IN SCHOOL AGAIN, ISN'T IT?
NO, IT'S GOING TO BE THE SAME AS ALWAYS!
SCHULZ

BEFORE THE BALL IS PITCHED, YOU SHOULD DECIDE WHAT YOU'RE GOING TO DO IF IT'S HIT TO YOU...
OKAY, I'VE DECIDED..
© 1986 United Feature Syndicate, Inc.
9-19
IF IT'S HIT TO ME, I'M GOING HOME!
SCHULZ

© 1986 United Feature Syndicate, Inc.
WHY DO I DO IT?
WHY DO I EAT THINGS LIKE THAT?
NOW I FEEL TERRIBLE.. I NEVER LEARN...
9-20
PIZZA A LA MODE
SCHULZ

"TO DIVIDE FRACTIONS, USE THE RECIPROCAL AND MULTIPLY"
© 1986 United Feature Syndicate, Inc.
9-22
WHY ?
WHY USE THE RECIPROCAL ?
NO, WHY WAS I BORN ?
SCHULZ

DID YOU KNOW I HAVE AN UNCLE WHO'S IN A STAGE PLAY ?
HE SAYS AN ACTOR'S BIGGEST FEAR IS BEING IN A TURKEY THAT FOLDS
© 1986 United Feature Syndicate, Inc.
9-23
HOW DO YOU FOLD A TURKEY ?
SCHULZ

PEANUTS
featuring
"Good ol' Charlie Brown"
by SCHULZ
" ♡ "
YOUR STORIES ARE DUMB!
THEY DON'T HAVE ENOUGH ROMANCE..
I'VE JUST BEEN READING A VERY ROMANTIC BOOK...

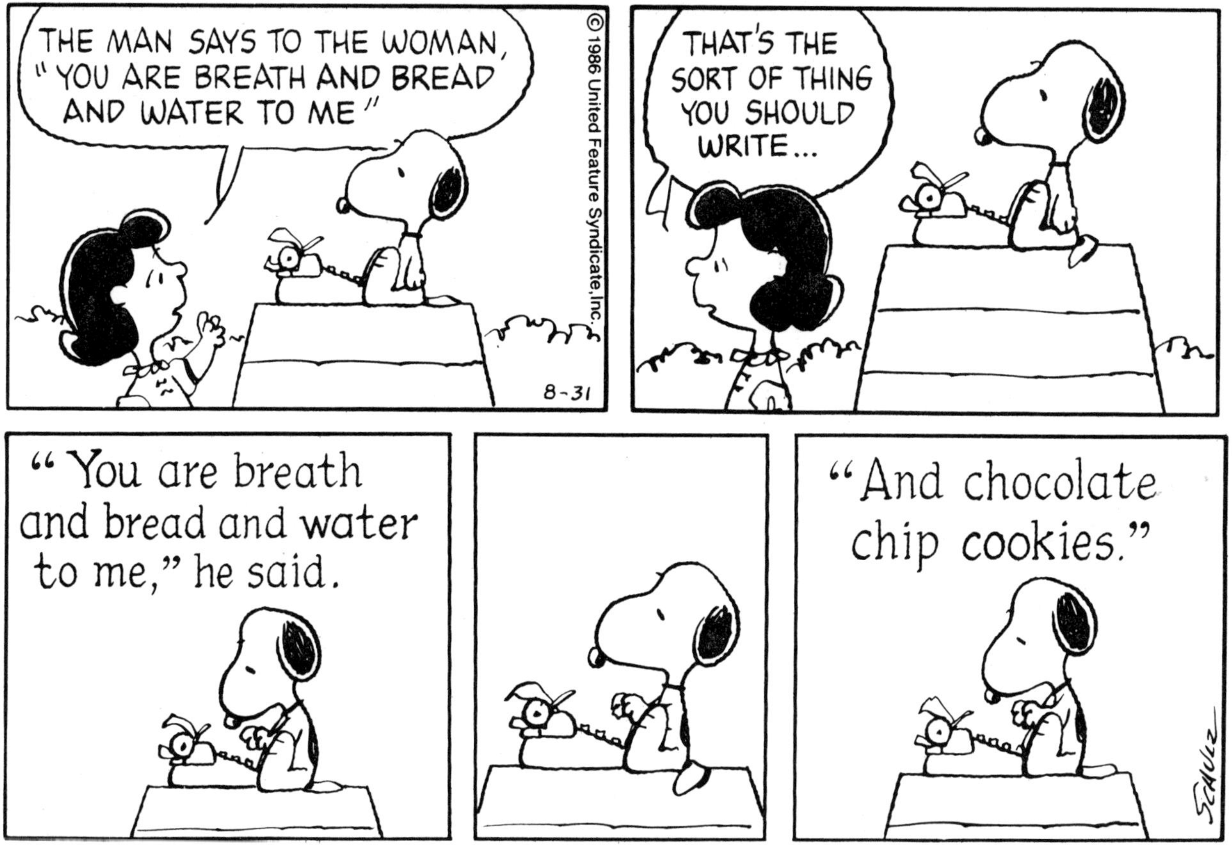
THE MAN SAYS TO THE WOMAN, "YOU ARE BREATH AND BREAD AND WATER TO ME"
© 1986 United Feature Syndicate, Inc.
8-31
THAT'S THE SORT OF THING YOU SHOULD WRITE...
"You are breath and bread and water to me," he said.
"And chocolate chip cookies."
SCHULZ

YES, MA'AM.. A REPORT ON THE FRENCH REVOLUTION..
© 1986 United Feature Syndicate, Inc.
TWO THOUSAND WORDS?
9-24
YES, MA'AM
PLEASE ALLOW FOUR TO SIX WEEKS FOR DELIVERY
SCHULZ

I ALMOST GOT YOU A BIRTHDAY CARD TODAY..
9-25
ALMOST?
I DIDN'T HAVE ENOUGH MONEY TO PAY FOR IT SO I LEFT IT AT THE STORE..
© 1986 United Feature Syndicate, Inc.
YOU CAN PICK IT UP AT "WILL CALL"
SCHULZ

DID YOU EVER GO TO PRE-SCHOOL, MARCIE?
SURE..WE DIDN'T DO MUCH THOUGH..JUST PLAYED AND ATE SNACKS...
© 1986 United Feature Syndicate,Inc.
9-26
IF I KNOW YOU, IT WAS A LOW CHOLESTEROL PRE-SCHOOL!
HA HA HA HA!
YOU'RE WEIRD, SIR..
SCHULZ

IT SAYS HERE THAT THE WORLD REVOLVES AROUND THE SUN ONCE A YEAR..
THE WORLD REVOLVES AROUND THE SUN?
© 1986 United Feature Syndicate,Inc.
ARE YOU SURE?
I THOUGHT IT REVOLVED AROUND ME!
SCHULZ
9-27

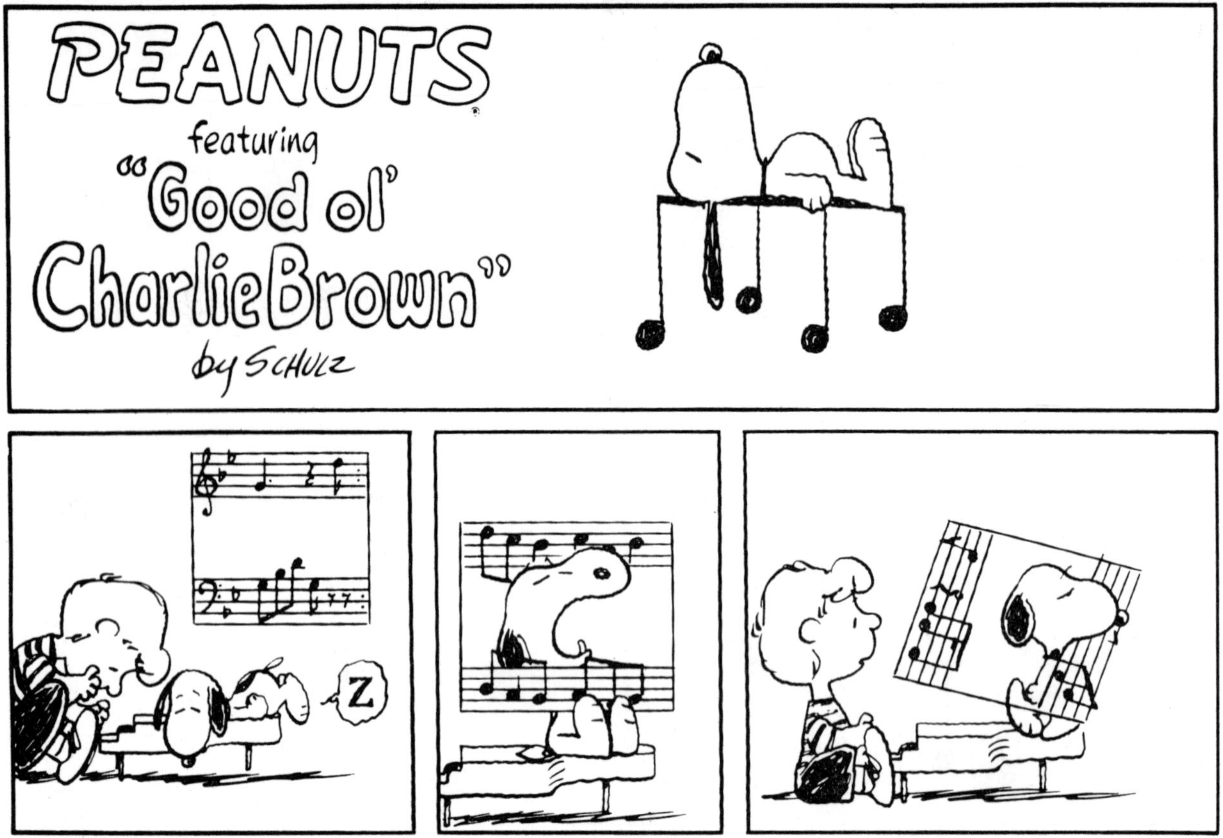
PEANUTS
featuring
"Good ol' Charlie Brown"
by SCHULZ
Z

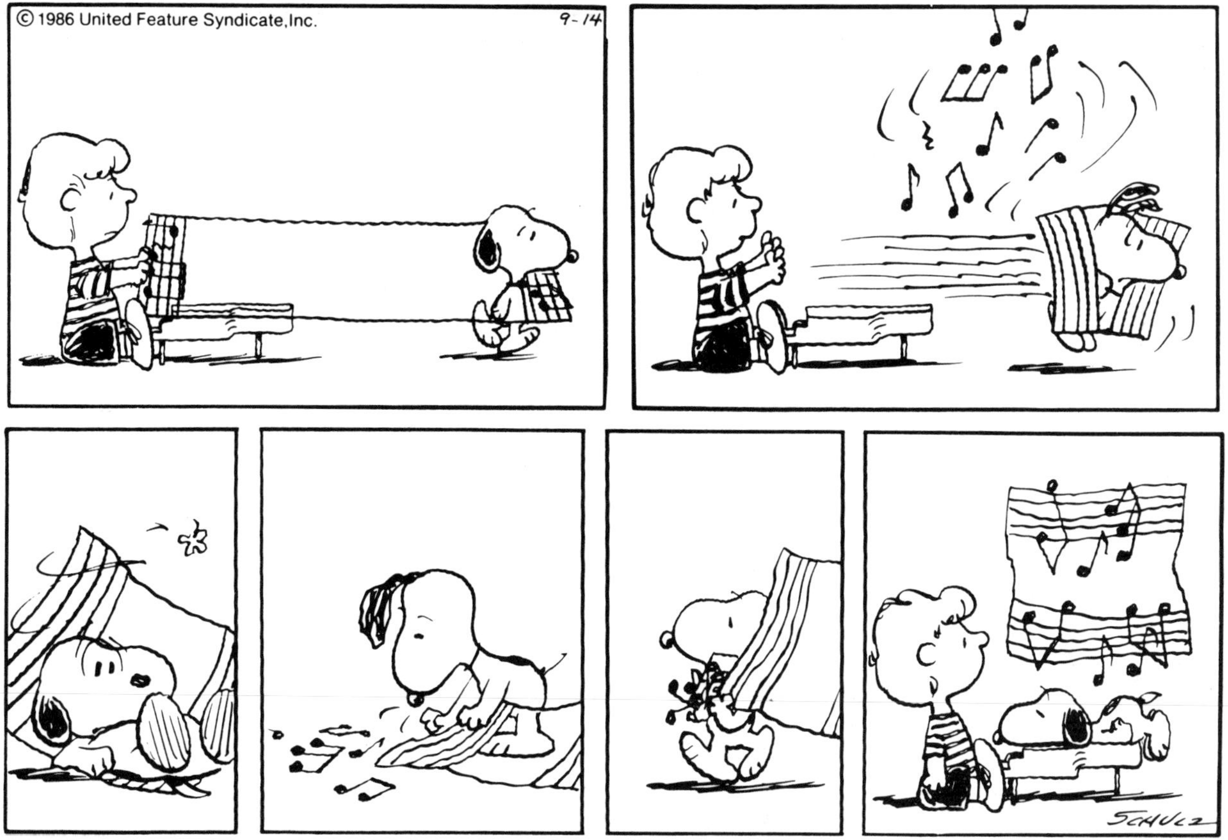
© 1986 United Feature Syndicate, Inc.
9-14
SCHULZ

LIFE IS STRANGE
YOU CAN BE VERY CLOSE TO SOMEONE..
THEN, FOR NO REASON AT ALL, YOU SEEM TO GRADUALLY DRIFT APART
MY SUPPER DISH USED TO BE TWO FEET AWAY.. NOW, IT'S THREE FEET
© 1986 United Feature Syndicate, Inc.
9-29

WATCH OUT, MARCIE.. YOU'RE GOING TO BUMP INTO MY DESK...
BUMP!
BEEP BEEP BEEP BEEP BEEP BEEP
SORRY, MA'AM..SHE SET OFF MY ALARM SYSTEM!
YOU REALLY ARE WEIRD, SIR!
© 1986 United Feature Syndicate, Inc.
9-30

10-1
NO!
© 1986 United Feature Syndicate, Inc.
I SAID WE'RE GOING OUT TO KICK AROUND THE OL' PIGSKIN..
I DIDN'T SAY "BEAGLESKIN"!

YOU'RE GOING TO BE PROUD OF ME, MARCIE
GUESS WHAT I HAVE IN MY LUNCH..AN APPLE!
9-18
WHERE IS IT? I KNOW I PUT IT IN HERE THIS MORNING...
© 1986 United Feature Syndicate, Inc.
HERE IT IS..UNDERNEATH ALL THE DOUGHNUTS!

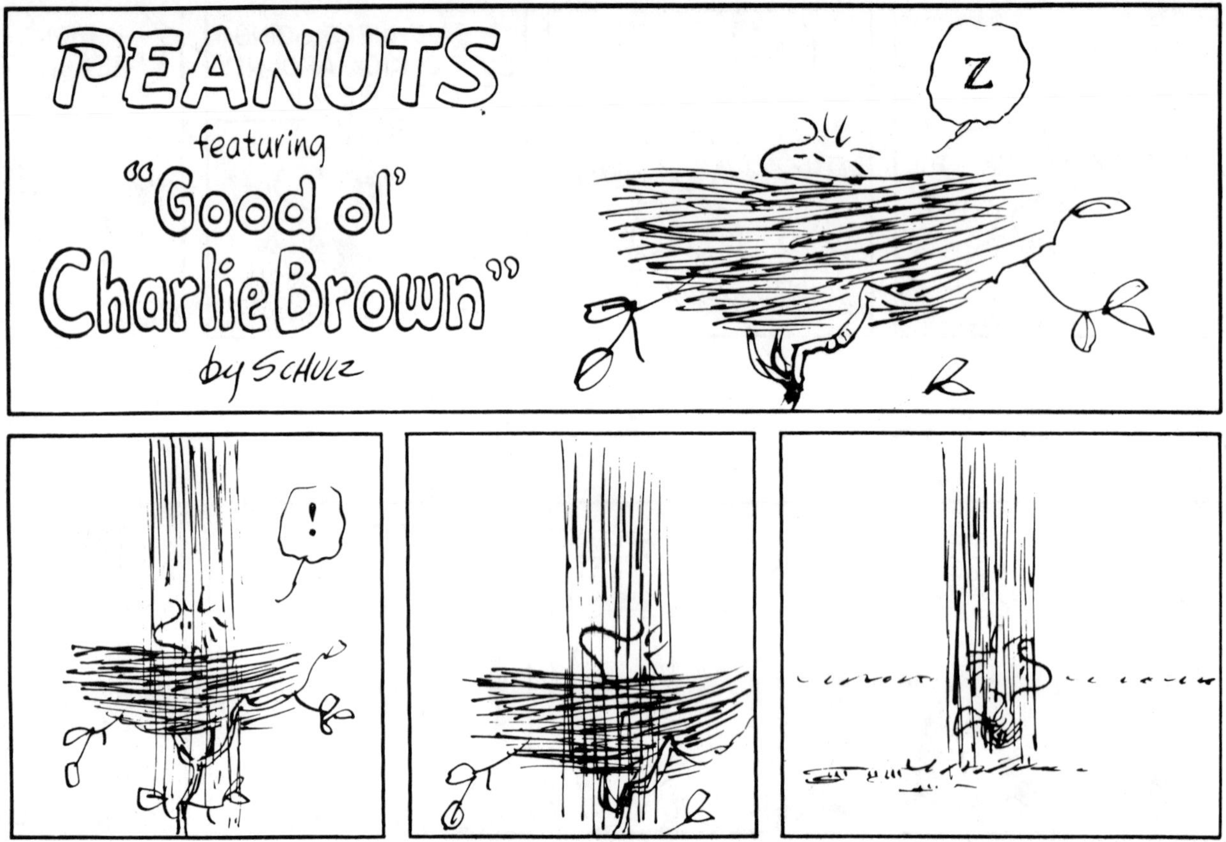
PEANUTS
featuring
"Good ol' Charlie Brown"
by SCHULZ
Z
!

© 1986 United Feature Syndicate, Inc.
9-28
?
I DON'T KNOW..
SOME CLOUDS ARE JUST KIND OF WEIRD...
AND THEY HATE TO BE CALLED WEIRD..
SCHULZ

THIS IS MY REPORT ON THE LIFE AND TIMES OF GEORGE WASHINGTON
WHEN WAS HE BORN? HE WAS BORN IN 1732
WHAT WAS HIS EARLY EDUCATION LIKE?
10-2
© 1986 United Feature Syndicate, Inc.
I'M SORRY.. WE HAVE NO HARD DATA ON THAT..
SCHULZ

"AND DIED IN 1799 SHORTLY AFTER AN EXHAUSTING HORSEBACK RIDE IN THE COLD"
THAT COMPLETES MY REPORT ON THE LIFE AND TIMES OF GEORGE WASHINGTON
10-3
BACK UP TO YOU, MA'AM..
SCHULZ
© 1986 United Feature Syndicate, Inc.

HERE'S THE WORLD WAR I FLYING ACE WALKING OUT TO HIS SOPWITH CAMEL..
AH! OUR SQUADRON COMMANDER IS ON THE FIELD..
10-4
NOW, THAT HURTS MY FEELINGS...
© 1986 United Feature Syndicate, Inc.
HE DIDN'T SAY, "HAPPY FLYING!"
SCHULZ

HERE'S THE WORLD WAR I FLYING ACE HIGH OVER ENEMY LINES...
10-6
SUDDENLY HE TURNS HIS PLANE AROUND!
SOMETHING IS CALLING HIM BACK...
© 1986 United Feature Syndicate, Inc.
DOUGHNUTS IN THE RED CROSS TENT!
SCHULZ

HERE'S THE WORLD WAR I FLYING ACE SEARCHING THE SKIES FOR HIS ENEMY, THE RED BARON..
10-7
DUCKING IN AND OUT OF THE CLOUDS, HE PLAYS A DANGEROUS GAME OF HIDE-AND-SEEK
PEEKABOO, I SEE YOU!
© 1986 United Feature Syndicate, Inc.
ACTUALLY, WORLD WAR I FLYING ACES VERY SELDOM SAID, "PEEKABOO, I SEE YOU!"
SCHULZ

HERE'S THE WORLD WAR I FLYING ACE ZOOMING OVER ENEMY LINES...
10-8
MACHINE GUNS BLAZING HE DIVES DOWN OUT OF THE CLOUDS...
OOOPS! SORRY..
© 1986 United Feature Syndicate, Inc.
I THINK I JUST SHOT A ZAMBONI!
SCHULZ

HERE'S THE WORLD WAR I FLYING ACE READING A LETTER FROM HIS SWEETHEART BACK HOME
"DEAR EX-BOYFRIEND, I AM GOING TO MARRY YOUR COUSIN...JUST THOUGHT YOU'D LIKE TO KNOW..."
10-9
"BEST REGARDS, YOUR EX-SWEETHEART"
© 1986 United Feature Syndicate, Inc.
"P.S. GOOD LUCK IN THE WAR"
SCHULZ

I CAN'T BELIEVE IT.. HERE I AM OVERSEAS FIGHTING IN THE WAR, AND WHAT HAPPENS?
10-10
© 1986 United Feature Syndicate, Inc.
MY GIRLFRIEND WRITES AND TELLS ME SHE'S GOING TO MARRY MY COUSIN!
I WONDER HOW LONG IT WILL TAKE ME TO FORGET HER...
THAT WASN'T TOO BAD.. I FORGOT HER IN FOURTEEN DOUGHNUTS!
SCHULZ

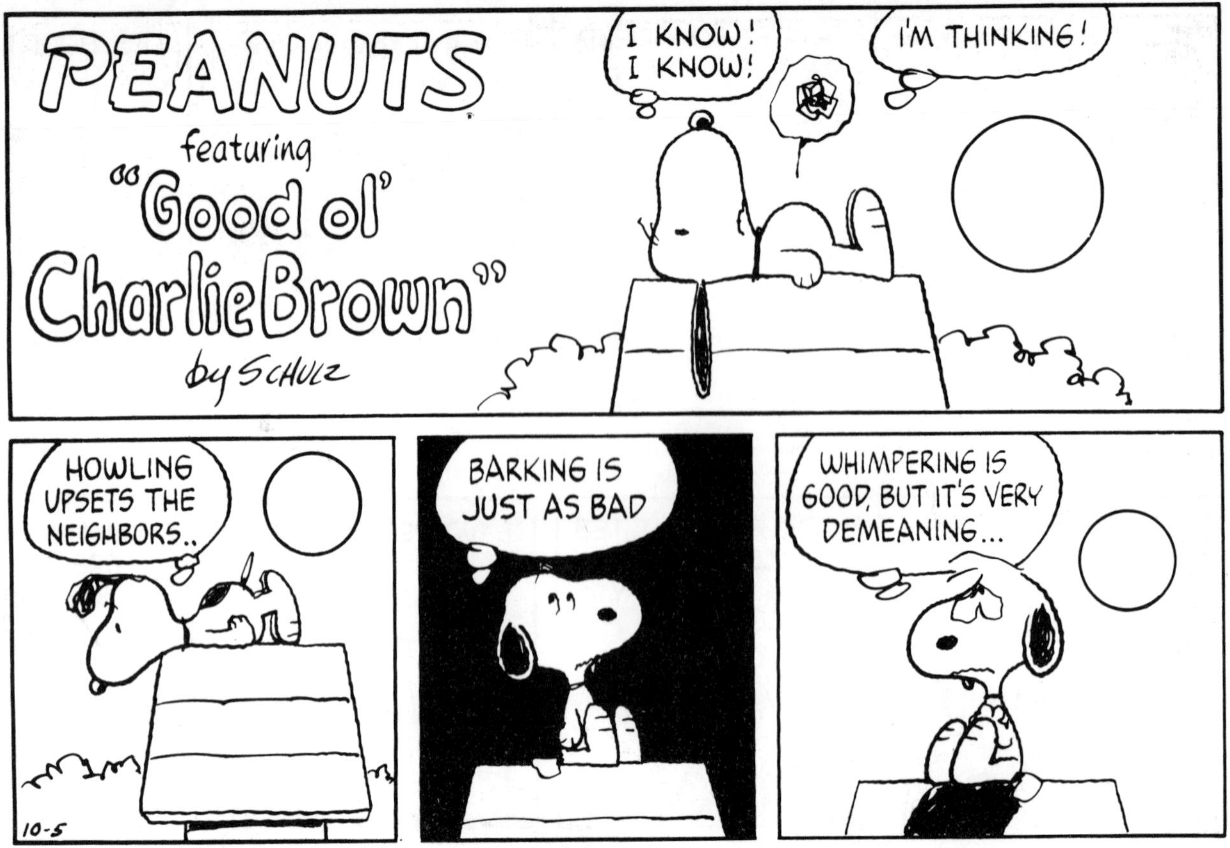
PEANUTS
featuring
"Good ol' Charlie Brown"
by SCHULZ
I KNOW! I KNOW!
I'M THINKING!
HOWLING UPSETS THE NEIGHBORS..
10-5
BARKING IS JUST AS BAD
WHIMPERING IS GOOD, BUT IT'S VERY DEMEANING...

KICKING THE BACK DOOR COULD SET OFF AN ALARM OR SOMETHING...
© 1986 United Feature Syndicate, Inc.
SO WHAT DOES THAT LEAVE?
THANK YOU
THE OL' CHOCOLATE CHIP COOKIE STARE!
SCHULZ

WE SHOULD ORGANIZE A FOOTBALL TEAM, MARCIE
10-14
WE CAN'T, SIR..WE DON'T HAVE COSTUMES
UNIFORMS
© 1986 United Feature Syndicate, Inc.
WHATEVER
SCHULZ

I DON'T WANT TO PLAY FOOTBALL, SIR..IT'S NOT FEMININE ENOUGH!
NOT FEMININE ENOUGH?!!
© 1986 United Feature Syndicate, Inc.
WHAT DO YOU WANT TO DO, TIE A RIBBON AROUND THE BALL OR SOMETHING?
10-15
LOOKS CUTE, DOESN'T IT?
SCHULZ

I'LL HOLD THE BALL, SIR, AND YOU KICK IT...
MARCIE, I'M NOT GONNA KICK A BALL THAT HAS A CUTE RIBBON TIED AROUND IT!
© 1986 United Feature Syndicate, Inc.
10-16
I'LL BET THE ICEBOX WOULD
"REFRIGERATOR"
WHATEVER
SCHULZ

AND MARCIE SAYS FOOTBALL ISN'T FEMININE, CHUCK.. ISN'T SHE SOMETHING?
IF I LIKE TO PLAY FOOTBALL, DOES THAT MEAN I'M NOT FEMININE, CHUCK?
© 1986 United Feature Syndicate, Inc.
WHAT DO YOU THINK, CHUCK? HUH? WHAT DO YOU THINK?
10/17
WE'RE SORRY.. THE NUMBER YOU HAVE REACHED IS NO LONGER IN SERVICE..
SCHULZ

PEANUTS
featuring "Good ol' Charlie Brown"
by SCHULZ
I SEE THEY HAVE BUTTER PECAN..
WHAT IF I ORDER IT, AND DON'T LIKE IT?
YOU COULD TRY PISTACHIO ALMOND
WHAT IF I ORDER IT, AND DON'T LIKE IT?
10-12

HOW ABOUT MINT CHOCOLATE CHIP ?
WHAT IF I ORDER IT, AND DON'T LIKE IT ?
I THINK I'D BETTER JUST HAVE VANILLA
WHAT'S THE MATTER ?
© 1986 United Feature Syndicate, Inc.
I DON'T LIKE IT !
SCHULZ

HERE'S AN ARTICLE ABOUT WHAT YOU SHOULD DO WITH YOUR BASEBALL GLOVE FOR THE WINTER...
" PUT YOUR GLOVE AWAY IN A DRY PLACE WHERE THE DOG CAN'T FIND IT "
10-20
© 1986 United Feature Syndicate, Inc.
" IF YOU'RE A DOG, PUT YOUR GLOVE AWAY IN A DRY PLACE WHERE THE KIDS CAN'T FIND IT "
SCHULZ

YES, MA'AM.. THIS IS MY REPORT ON THE MUSIC CONCERT.. IT WAS VERY BEAUTIFUL...
IT WAS THE FIRST TIME I EVER HEARD A VEAL PICCATA...
BACH TOCCATA
WHATEVER
10-21
SCHULZ
© 1986 United Feature Syndicate, Inc.

THIS IS THE POEM I HAVE MEMORIZED..
10-22
"FOG" BY CARL SANDBURG
© 1986 United Feature Syndicate, Inc.
OKAY! START THE POTS!
JUST A LITTLE SPECIAL EFFECT, MA'AM..
SCHULZ

IT'S GRATIFYING TO HAVE A DOG GREET YOU WHEN YOU GET HOME FROM SCHOOL..
10-23
SIGH
SCHULZ
© 1986 United Feature Syndicate, Inc.

I JUST GOT BACK FROM THE DENTIST
© 1986 United Feature Syndicate,Inc.
I'M SO HAPPY..HE SAID I HAVE A NICE BITE!
10-24
GOOD FOR YOU
IF A DOG HAS A NICE BITE, HE JUST GETS YELLED AT!

SEE THAT SQUIRREL? HE'S BEEN STORING UP FOOD FOR THE WINTER..
I'LL BET YOU NEVER THINK ABOUT THAT, DO YOU?
COME ON, TELL ME.. WHAT HAVE YOU DONE TO PREPARE FOR WINTER?
10-18
© 1986 United Feature Syndicate,Inc.

© 1986 United Feature Syndicate,Inc.
HELLO?
10-11
SURE..GO RIGHT AHEAD..
WHO CARES? HOW SHOULD I KNOW?
I LOVE OPINION POLLS!
SCHULZ

RATS!
I HAVE AN "EDUCATED SLICE," BUT IT ONLY WENT TO THE THIRD GRADE!
10-27 © 1986 United Feature Syndicate,Inc.
SCHULZ

PEANUTS
featuring "Good ol' Charlie Brown"
by SCHULZ
ONCE A YEAR..JUST ONCE A YEAR..
CHARLIE BROWN, I'LL HOLD THE BALL, AND YOU COME RUNNING UP AND KICK IT!
SURE! SURE I WILL! YOU MUST THINK I'M REALLY STUPID!
10-19
© 1986 United Feature Syndicate, Inc.
PLEASE, CHARLIE BROWN..I LOOK FORWARD TO THIS SPECIAL MOMENT ALL YEAR...

I SUPPOSE IF SOMEONE LOOKS FORWARD TO SOMETHING, IT'S WRONG TO SPOIL IT..
THIS YEAR I'M GONNA KICK THAT BALL CLEAR TO BULLHEAD CITY!
AAUGH!
WHAM!
HOW DEPRESSING... YOU LOOK FORWARD ALL YEAR TO A SPECIAL MOMENT, AND BEFORE YOU KNOW IT, IT'S OVER!
IT'S SO DEPRESSING
I CAN'T STAND IT!
SCHULZ

Dear Snoopy,
Our cactus club had its annual marshmallow roast last night.
I was the only member who showed up.
Which was fortunate
Because we only had one marshmallow.
10-28
© 1986 United Feature Syndicate, Inc.
SCHULZ

WIND IS DISTURBING TO ANIMALS WHO LIVE IN THE DESERT..
A LOT OF ANIMALS WON'T COME OUT OF THEIR HOLES IF IT'S WINDY...
WHEN THE WIND IS BLOWING, THEY CAN'T HEAR PREDATORS..
IT ALSO BLOWS YOUR HAT OFF!
© 1986 United Feature Syndicate, Inc.
10-29
SCHULZ

Dear Grampa and Grandma, Thank you for the Christmas present.
© 1986 United Feature Syndicate, Inc.
GETTING ALL YOUR "THANK YOU'S" WRITTEN AHEAD OF TIME, I SEE...
OR ARE THESE FOR LAST YEAR? HA HA HA HA!!
THESE ARE FOR 1980!
10-30
SCHULZ

Dear Snoopy,
10-31
© 1986 United Feature Syndicate, Inc.
Just a few lines to let you know what our cactus club has been doing.
Last night we had a new kind of marshmallow roast.
We all sat around and insulted a marshmallow.
SCHULZ

PEANUTS

featuring "Good ol' Charlie Brown"

by Schulz

AND I DID IT MY WAY!

ON HALLOWEEN, THE GREAT PUMPKIN RISES FROM THE PUMPKIN PATCH AND FLIES THROUGH THE AIR WITH TOYS FOR ALL THE CHILDREN IN THE WORLD!

I BELIEVE YOU

AND YOU KNOW WHAT HAPPENS ON SECRETARIES DAY?

THE GREAT SECRETARY RISES FROM HER DESK AND RIDES THROUGH THE CITY IN A TAXICAB WITH NOTE PADS FOR ALL THE SECRETARIES EVERYWHERE!
AND ON GRANDPARENTS DAY, THE GREAT GRANDMOTHER RISES OUT OF HER CONDOMINIUM WITH COOKIES FOR ALL THE GRANDCHILDREN IN THE WORLD!
HA HA HA HA!
10-26
WAIT! LET ME TELL YOU ABOUT MOTHER-IN-LAW'S DAY! WHERE'D HE GO?
SCHULZ

HI, MY NAME IS TAPIOCA PUDDING
I KNOW
© 1986 United Feature Syndicate, Inc.
MY DAD IS IN LICENSING.. MY PICTURE IS GOING TO BE ON GREETING CARDS, T-SHIRTS AND EVERYTHING!
11-3
WOULDN'T YOU LIKE TO HAVE A LUNCH BOX WITH MY PICTURE ON IT?
WHAT'S WRONG WITH THE PICTURE ON THIS LUNCH BOX?
MICE DON'T HAVE BIG ROUND EARS!
SCHULZ

I HAVE A THEORY, MARCIE..
I THINK YOUR WHOLE BODY BECOMES SUSPICIOUS WHEN YOU'RE NOT READY FOR A TEST..
AND WHEN YOU LOOK AT THE QUESTIONS...
YOUR HAIR IS THE FIRST TO KNOW!
© 1986 United Feature Syndicate, Inc.
11-4

YES, SIR.. I'D LIKE TO BUY A DOZEN GOLF BALLS FOR MY DAD... IT'S HIS BIRTHDAY..
SA
11-5
HE ALWAYS YELLS AT THE BALL..
"GO! STOP! RUN! BITE! COME BACK!"
© 1986 United Feature Syndicate, Inc.
DO YOU HAVE ANY THAT LISTEN?
SCHULZ

I WONDER WHAT WOULD HAPPEN IF I WINKED AT THAT LITTLE RED-HAIRED GIRL...
NOTHING
© 1986 United Feature Syndicate, Inc.
11-6
PROBABLY BECAUSE SHE ISN'T HERE TODAY..
SCHULZ

YES, MA'AM..I KNOW THE ANSWER...
THE ANSWER IS... UH..IS...UH..IS...
11-7
UH...
© 1986 United Feature Syndicate, Inc.
WHY DON'T WE JUST KEEP IT OUR LITTLE SECRET?
SCHULZ

I LOVE DANCES
© 1986 United Feature Syndicate, Inc.
BUT WHO WANTS TO DANCE WITH A DOG?
NOBODY!
I HATE BEING A WALLBEAGLE!
11-8
SCHULZ

HI! MY NAME IS TAPIOCA PUDDING!
I KNOW
BUS
MY DAD IS IN LICENSING..MY PICTURE IS GOING TO BE ON EVERY PRODUCT IN THE COUNTRY..
© 1986 United Feature Syndicate, Inc.
DO YOU THINK YOU AND I HAVE MUCH IN COMMON?
I DON'T KNOW
11-10
DO YOU LIKE UP-FRONT MONEY?
SCHULZ

EVERY VETERANS DAY I GO OVER TO BILL MAULDIN'S HOUSE..
11-11
WE QUAFF A FEW ROOT BEERS AND TELL WAR STORIES..
I'LL PROBABLY BE HOME EARLY...
© 1986 United Feature Syndicate, Inc.
OL' BILL CAN'T STAY AWAKE AS LATE AS HE USED TO..
SCHULZ

PEANUTS
featuring
"Good ol' Charlie Brown"
by SCHULZ
© 1986 United Feature Syndicate, Inc.
BONK!

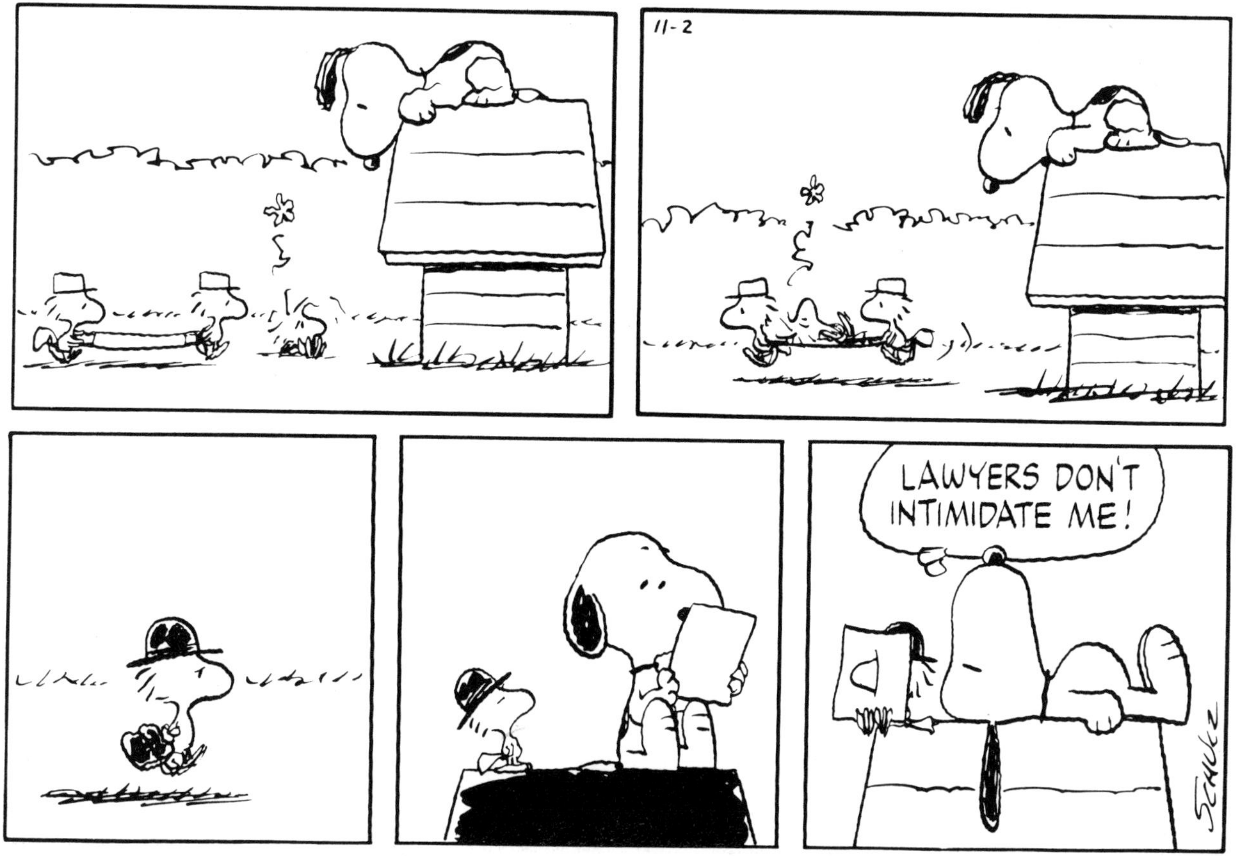
11-2
LAWYERS DON'T INTIMIDATE ME!
SCHULZ

MA'AM?
MARCIE SAYS YOU GAVE HER AN "A" ON HER PAPER...
© 1986 United Feature Syndicate, Inc.
YOU COULD'VE GOT THE SAME PAPER FROM ME FOR A "D-MINUS"
11-12
WHY PAY FULL PRICE?
SCHULZ

SOME PEOPLE STAY IN THE SAME PLACE ALL THEIR LIVES
NOT ME.. WHEN I GROW UP, I'M GONNA MOVE ON!
© 1986 United Feature Syndicate, Inc.
YOU'RE NOT GONNA CATCH ME LIVING HERE FOR THE REST OF MY LIFE..
YOU DON'T LIKE IT HERE?
WHERE ARE WE?
SCHULZ
11-13

PSYCHIATRIC HELP 5¢
THE DOCTOR IS IN
THINK ABOUT WHAT I'VE SAID, CHARLIE BROWN
IT'S REALLY ALL UP TO YOU..
THE DOCTOR IS IN
11-14
FIVE CENTS, PLEASE
THE DOCTOR IS IN
DO YOU TAKE BUBBLE GUM CARDS?
THE DOCTOR IS IN
SCHULZ
© 1986 United Feature Syndicate, Inc.

EVERY NIGHT MY SUPPER COMES THROUGH THAT BACK DOOR..
SURPRISE!
TONIGHT I WENT OUT THE FRONT DOOR AND CAME AROUND THE SIDE OF THE HOUSE..
I'LL EAT FIRST, AND THEN I'LL CALL THE HUMANE SOCIETY!
SCHULZ
11-15
© 1986 United Feature Syndicate, Inc.

PEANUTS
featuring
"Good ol' Charlie Brown"
by SCHULZ
DRESSING ROOM
HERE'S THE WORLD FAMOUS HOCKEY PLAYER SITTING IN THE DRESSING ROOM BEFORE THE GAME..
HE IS VERY NERVOUS

© 1986 United Feature Syndicate, Inc.
HE NEEDS TO DO SOMETHING TO CALM HIS NERVES...
11-9
HE DECIDES TO TAPE HIS STICK..
TAPING YOUR STICK HELPS TO RELIEVE THE TENSION
SCHULZ
UNLESS YOU'RE SO NERVOUS YOU TAPE YOURSELF TO THE BENCH!

WE START OUR HIKE IN EXACTLY ONE HOUR
I SUGGEST YOU GET YOUR GEAR TOGETHER RIGHT NOW..
© 1986 United Feature Syndicate, Inc.
AND REMEMBER, ALL WE'RE TAKING WITH US ARE THE NECESSITIES OF LIFE!
11-17
SCHULZ

I LOVE NATURE BOOKS
© 1986 United Feature Syndicate, Inc.
HERE'S AN INTERESTING ITEM..
"A CODFISH MAY LAY AS MANY AS NINE MILLION EGGS AT ONE TIME"
!!!! !!!?
NO, CONRAD.. IT DOESN'T SAY WHO COUNTED THEM
SCHULZ
11-18

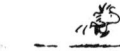

OKAY, TROOPS, HERE WE GO OFF INTO THE WILDERNESS..
AS WE MARCH ALONG, IF YOU HAVE ANY QUESTIONS, DON'T HESITATE TO ASK...
11-19
© 1986 United Feature Syndicate, Inc.
NO, OLIVIER, I DOUBT THAT WE'LL SEE ANY SOUVENIR STANDS!
SCHULZ

WHAT? WHERE?
11-20
HEY! WHAT'RE YOU DOING? COME BACK!
I WAS WRONG..
© 1986 United Feature Syndicate, Inc.
WE DID PASS A SOUVENIR STAND!
SCHULZ

I'M ASHAMED OF YOU GUYS
WE DON'T GO ON A NATURE HIKE JUST TO SPEND ALL OUR TIME AT A SOUVENIR STAND!
I'LL BET HARRIET DIDN'T STUFF HER BACKPACK WITH A LOT OF USELESS SOUVENIRS...
SCHULZ
11-21
© 1986 United Feature Syndicate, Inc.

WHILE WE'RE OUT HERE, WE REALLY SHOULD DO SOME BIRD WATCHING..
CONRAD WATCHES BILL, WHO WATCHES HARRIET, WHO WATCHES WOODSTOCK, WHO WATCHES OLIVIER, WHO WATCHES CONRAD!
11-22
HA HA HA HA!
BIRDS HAVE NO SENSE OF HUMOR
SCHULZ
© 1986 United Feature Syndicate, Inc.

I'M GOING OVER TO THE BAKERY IN A FEW MINUTES...
11-24
IF THERE'S ANYTHING YOU'D LIKE, LET ME KNOW..
I HAVE SOME FREE TIME THIS AFTERNOON..
HOW ABOUT AN HOUR'S WORTH OF DOUGHNUTS?
SCHULZ
© 1986 United Feature Syndicate, Inc.

MARCIE, DO YOU THINK THE TEACHER GRADES OUR PAPERS ON NEATNESS?
ABSOLUTELY..FOR INSTANCE, THE WAY YOU REMOVE A PIECE OF PAPER FROM YOUR BINDER...
11-25
YOU SHOULD ALWAYS OPEN THE RINGS.. NOT JUST TEAR IT OUT...
© 1986 United Feature Syndicate, Inc.
ANOTHER D-MINUS!
SCHULZ

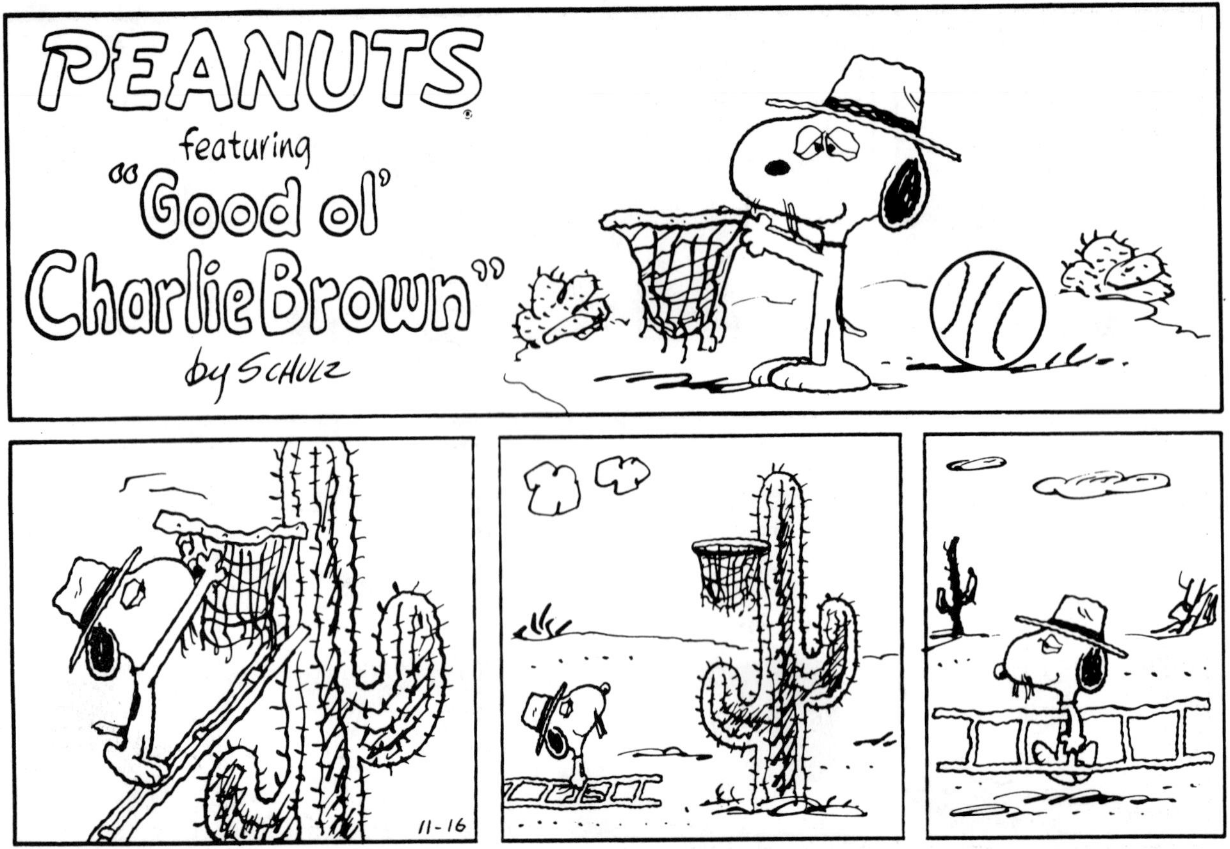
PEANUTS®
featuring "Good ol' Charlie Brown"
by SCHULZ
11-16

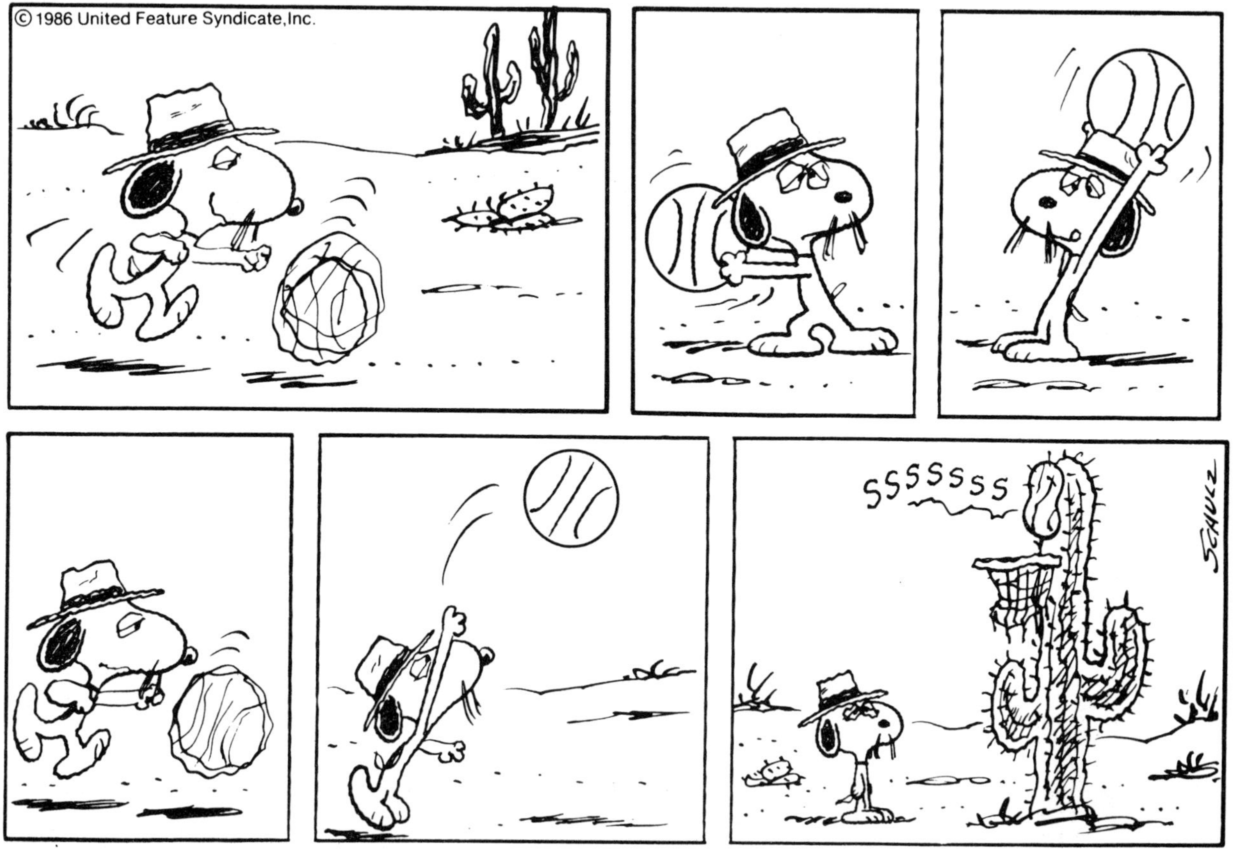
© 1986 United Feature Syndicate, Inc.
SSSSSSSS
SCHULZ

11-26
© 1986 United Feature Syndicate, Inc.
BOY, HAVE WE GOT BAD NEWS FOR YOU TONIGHT!
HOW BAD IS IT?
WE'RE NOT EVEN GOING TO GIVE YOU THE DETAILS AT ELEVEN!
SCHULZ

TODAY IS THANKSGIVING
I THINK IT WOULD BE NICE IF YOU WERE TO SHARE YOUR DINNER WITH THE CAT NEXT DOOR
11-27
HOW WOULD YOU LIKE TO DO IT?
ON THE END OF A LONG STICK!
SCHULZ
© 1986 United Feature Syndicate, Inc.

Dear Santa
© 1986 United Feature Syndicate, Inc. 11-28
WHO'S "SANTA SMUDGE"?
SCHULZ

HERE'S THE WORLD FAMOUS HOCKEY PLAYER RACING DOWN THE ICE!
© 1986 United Feature Syndicate, Inc.
11-29
HE FAKES A SLAPSHOT..
BUT IT DOESN'T FAZE THE GOALIE..
HE KNOWS I DON'T HAVE A SLAPSHOT..
SCHULZ

PEANUTS
featuring
"Good ol' Charlie Brown"
by SCHULZ
HEY, SNOOPY, LET'S GO FOR A WALK!
© 1986 United Feature Syndicate, Inc.
THIS IS THE WAY IT WAS MEANT TO BE

A BOY AND HIS DOG HIKING LIKE PERFECT COMRADES THROUGH THE WOODS
IF YOU SEE A SQUIRREL, OR A DEER, OR A PHEASANT OR A RABBIT, PLEASE FEEL FREE TO BARK AND HOWL AND PURSUE THEM MADLY OVER THE HILLS, THROUGH THE STREAMS AND ACROSS THE FIELDS!
12-14
I HATE IT WHEN HE LOOKS AT ME LIKE THAT..
SCHULZ

HI! MY NAME IS TAPIOCA PUDDING
I KNOW
MY DAD IS IN LICENSING.. MY PICTURE IS GOING TO BE ON GREETING CARDS AND LUNCH BOXES
12-1
© 1986 United Feature Syndicate, Inc.
IF YOU WERE MY BOYFRIEND, YOU WOULDN'T HAVE TO CARRY MY PICTURE IN YOUR WALLET..
IT WOULD ALREADY BE ON YOUR LUNCH BOX!
I CAN'T STAND IT!
SCHULZ

DID BEETHOVEN EVER BUY HIS GIRLFRIEND FUZZY MITTENS FOR CHRISTMAS?
I DOUBT IT..
HERE'S YOUR CHANCE TO DO SOMETHING HE NEVER DID...
I'VE ALREADY THOUGHT OF DOING SOMETHING HE NEVER DID...
12-2
© 1986 United Feature Syndicate, Inc.
KLUNK!
SCHULZ

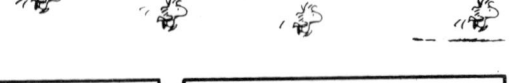

YES, MA'AM.. WE ENJOYED THE CONCERT
MARCIE SPENT THE WHOLE TIME FLAUTING WITH THE FLIRTIST...
FLIRTING WITH THE FLAUTIST
WHATEVER
12-3
SCHULZ
© 1986 United Feature Syndicate, Inc.

HOLD REAL STILL, PLEASE
12-4
OKAY, YOU CAN RELAX..
SCHULZ
© 1986 United Feature Syndicate, Inc.

SORRY, MA'AM..I DIDN'T MEAN TO BE LATE...
AND I DIDN'T MEAN TO FORGET MY HOMEWORK
AND I DIDN'T MEAN TO BE THE CAUSE OF YOUR HAIR TURNING WHAT APPEARS TO BE PREMATURELY GRAY..
12-5
© 1986 United Feature Syndicate, Inc.
I ALSO DIDN'T MEAN TO SAY THAT..
SCHULZ

ONE THING THAT MAKES DOGS SUPERIOR IS OUR ABILITY TO RAISE OUR EARS..
LIKE THIS, SEE?
12-6
ANOTHER THING THAT MAKES DOGS SUPERIOR IS..
© 1986 United Feature Syndicate, Inc.
WAIT! I WAS GOING TO TELL YOU ABOUT OUR NATURAL HUMILITY..
SCHULZ

WATCHING YOUR BLANKET TUMBLING AROUND IN THE DRYER IS SCARY...
WHAT IF IT NEVER COMES OUT? WHAT IF IT'S DESTROYED?
12-8
I SHOULDN'T BE WATCHING..
© 1986 United Feature Syndicate, Inc.
IT'S NOT SUITABLE VIEWING FOR CHILDREN..
SCHULZ

PARDON ME, SIR
© 1986 United Feature Syndicate, Inc.
A RECENT REPORT SHOWED THAT MANY ATTORNEYS ARE NO LONGER PRACTICING LAW
HAVE YOU FOUND ANYTHING THAT IS MORE IMPORTANT TO YOU THAN PRACTICING LAW?
12-9
EATING!
SCHULZ

PEANUTS
featuring "Good ol' Charlie Brown"
by SCHULZ
GATE 3
I DON'T CARE! IT'S NOT FAIR!
I WANNA ASK YOU SOMETHING! DO YOU REMEMBER BEFORE WE WERE BORN?
NOT HARDLY
WEREN'T WE UP IN HEAVEN WITH A BUNCH OF OTHER KIDS WAITING TO BE BORN?

THE THEOLOGICAL IMPLICATIONS OF THAT ARE WAY BEYOND ME..
WELL, DO YOU THINK WE EVER ASKED ABOUT BEING BORN?
I DON'T RECALL EVER ASKING ANYONE OR EVEN SEEING ANYONE...
SO YOU'RE SURE WE NEVER ASKED TO BE BORN?
11-23
NO, I DON'T THINK SO
YOU'RE SURE?
I'M POSITIVE
THAT'S WHAT I THOUGHT.. I JUST WANTED TO BE SURE...
© 1986 United Feature Syndicate, Inc.
I DIDN'T ASK TO BE BORN!!
SCHULZ

GUESS WHAT, CHUCK..
© 1986 United Feature Syndicate, Inc.
12-10
WE HAD A SPELLING TEST AT SCHOOL TODAY, AND I GOT A PERFECT SCORE!
GOOD FOR YOU..WHAT DID YOUR TEACHER SAY?
SHE ASKED ME TO FILL OUT AN ACCIDENT REPORT!
SCHULZ

12-11
EVERY TIME I LISTEN TO YOU, I'M REMINDED OF THAT OLD SAYING, "TALK IS CHEEP!"
HAHAHAHA!
© 1986 United Feature Syndicate, Inc.
SCHULZ

DO YOU EVER HEAR SOMETHING IN YOUR HEAD THAT WON'T GO AWAY?
YOU KNOW, LIKE A TUNE OR A CERTAIN PHRASE?
WHERE'S THAT STUPID BROTHER OF MINE?!
ALL THE TIME..
SCHULZ
12-12
© 1986 United Feature Syndicate, Inc.

Dear Santa Claus,
I hope this letter reaches you before Christmas.
I am worried about something.
When you come to fill my stocking...
Please be careful.
Love,
Spike
SCHULZ
12-13
© 1986 United Feature Syndicate, Inc.

PEANUTS
featuring "Good ol' Charlie Brown"
by SCHULZ
MOM SAYS IT'S BEDTIME!
"THIS IS A LIMITED OFFER..CALL NOW"
"OUR OPERATORS ARE STANDING BY"
© 1986 United Feature Syndicate, Inc.

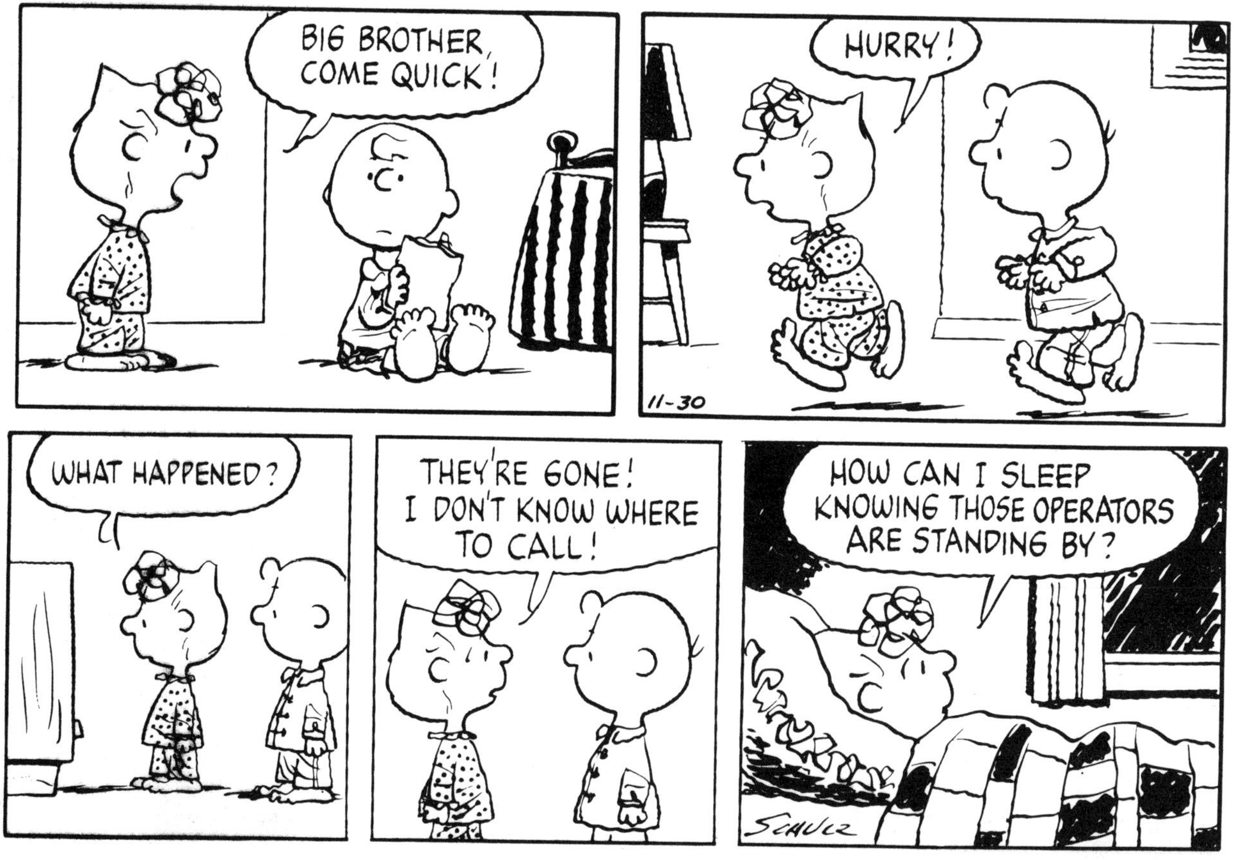
BIG BROTHER, COME QUICK!
HURRY!
11-30
WHAT HAPPENED?
THEY'RE GONE! I DON'T KNOW WHERE TO CALL!
HOW CAN I SLEEP KNOWING THOSE OPERATORS ARE STANDING BY?
SCHULZ

12-15
© 1986 United Feature Syndicate, Inc.
EIGHT BALL IN THE CORNER? YOU'RE KIDDING..
HA! YOU MISSED!
NEVER PLAY POOL WITH A SORE LOSER!
SCHULZ

© 1986 United Feature Syndicate, Inc.
MA'AM?
I WAS WONDERING IF YOU'D LET US MAKE SOME PAPER CHAINS FOR OUR CHRISTMAS TREE..
YOU KNOW, AS SORT OF A CLASS PROJECT..
12-16
WE COULD START WITH MY MATH PAPER..
SCHULZ

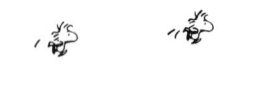

ANOTHER BIG HOCKEY GAME TODAY..
© 1986 United Feature Syndicate, Inc.
12-17
SOMEHOW, WE ALWAYS END UP PLAYING ON WOODSTOCK'S HOME ICE
IT WOULDN'T BE SO BAD EXCEPT FOR ONE THING..
HE NEVER LETS ME DRIVE THE ZAMBONI !
SCHULZ

HOW WAS SCHOOL TODAY?
WHO CARES?
I WAS JUST ASKING
IT'S MY NEW PHILOSOPHY... "WHO CARES?"
FROM NOW ON, NOTHING BOTHERS ME
10-13
WHO CARES? WHO CARES? WHO CARES?
SCHULZ
© 1986 United Feature Syndicate, Inc.

PEANUTS®
featuring
"Good ol' Charlie Brown"
by SCHULZ
Class of 1980
HOW DO I LOOK?
VERY NICE
WHERE ARE YOU GOING?
OUR KINDERGARTEN CLASS IS HAVING A REUNION..

IT SHOULD BE INTERESTING TO SEE HOW MUCH EVERYONE HAS CHANGED..
© 1986 United Feature Syndicate, Inc. 12-7
WELL, HOW WAS THE REUNION?
FINE! I HAD A GOOD TIME.. IT WAS NICE SEEING EVERYONE AGAIN
BUT YOU KNOW WHAT SURPRISED ME? NONE OF THE GUYS WERE BALD!
SCHULZ

I'M GOING OUT TO FALL DOWN A CHRISTMAS TREE
12-18
YOU MEAN CUT DOWN
I DON'T KNOW HOW TO CUT DOWN A CHRISTMAS TREE..
© 1986 United Feature Syndicate, Inc.
WHEN I LOOK AT IT, I HOPE IT'LL JUST FALL DOWN
SCHULZ

HEY, KID, WHAT'RE YOU DOIN' IN OUR YARD?!
12-19
© 1986 United Feature Syndicate, Inc.
YOU WEREN'T THINKIN' OF CUTTIN' THAT TREE DOWN WERE YA?
I DON'T KNOW HOW TO CUT A TREE DOWN..
WHAT IF IT JUST FALLS DOWN?
HA! IF IT FALLS DOWN, YOU CAN HAVE IT!
KLUNK!
I'LL TAKE IT!!
SCHULZ

HEY, KID.. YOU GOT A SISTER OR SOMETHING WITH YELLOW HAIR?
© 1986 United Feature Syndicate, Inc.
SHE STOLE A CHRISTMAS TREE FROM OUR YARD
12-20
I DIDN'T STEAL IT.. HE SAID IF IT FELL OVER, I COULD HAVE IT... WHEN I LOOKED AT IT, IT FELL OVER..
IT WAS A CHRISTMAS MIRACLE!

WHAT ARE YOU STANDING ON OUR PORCH FOR? GO HOME!
I WANT OUR TREE BACK!
YOU SAID IF IT FELL OVER, I COULD HAVE IT!
12-22
NOW, GET OFF OUR PORCH, OR I'LL CALL THE DOG!
© 1986 United Feature Syndicate, Inc.
DON'T CALL THE DOG.. HE'S DECORATING THE TREE..

I CAN'T SLEEP, BIG BROTHER..DO YOU THINK I SHOULD GIVE THE TREE BACK TO THAT UGLY KID?
WHY? ARE YOU STARTING TO FEEL GUILTY?
NO!
© 1986 United Feature Syndicate, Inc.
HE SAID I COULD HAVE THE TREE IF IT FELL OVER.. I DON'T FEEL GUILTY AT ALL!
TOMORROW IS CHRISTMAS EVE..
NOW, I FEEL GUILTY..
SCHULZ
12-23

HI! WE BROUGHT YOUR TREE BACK!
© 1986 United Feature Syndicate, Inc.
NO, KEEP IT! I WAS WRONG..IT'S YOURS! I SAID IF IT FELL OVER, IT WAS YOURS..KEEP IT!
REALLY? THANK YOU! MERRY CHRISTMAS!
12-24
NOW I HAVE TO DECORATE IT ALL OVER AGAIN
SCHULZ

MY GRANDFATHER LOVES TO SING HYMNS
HE CAN REMEMBER THE WORDS TO OVER A HUNDRED HYMNS!
7-18
© 1986 United Feature Syndicate, Inc.
DOES HE SING IN THE CHOIR?
NO, HE CAN'T REMEMBER WHERE THE CHURCH IS..
SCHULZ

HI, FRANKLIN! ABOUT THIS "WAR AND PEACE" WE'RE SUPPOSED TO READ DURING VACATION...
WHY DON'T WE SORT OF COOPERATE? YOU READ "WAR"... MARCIE CAN READ "PEACE"
WHAT WILL YOU READ?
12-29
"AND"!
© 1986 United Feature Syndicate, Inc.
SCHULZ

PEANUTS
featuring
"Good ol' CharlieBrown"
by SCHULZ
?
WHERE ARE ALL THE CANDY CANES?
THE WHAT?

THE CANDY CANES THAT WERE ON THE TREE..THEY'RE GONE!
12-28
© 1986 United Feature Syndicate, Inc.
HAVE YOU LOOKED OUTSIDE?
OUTSIDE?
SCHULZ

12-25
© 1986 United Feature Syndicate, Inc.
YOU CAN STOP STARING AT THE BACK DOOR.. ALL THE CHRISTMAS COOKIES ARE GONE!
I DIDN'T WANT YOU TO WASTE A GOOD STARE
HOW THOUGHTFUL
SCHULZ

Dear Gramma,
Thank you for the very nice Christmas present.
12-26
It was just what I wanted.
What was it?
SCHULZ
© 1986 United Feature Syndicate, Inc.

ON YOUR WAY TO THE COURTHOUSE, I SEE
I IMAGINE YOU'RE QUITE WELL KNOWN AMONG YOUR FELLOW ATTORNEYS
12-30
IS IT TRUE THAT THEY'VE GIVEN YOU A NICKNAME?
© 1986 United Feature Syndicate, Inc.
"JOE BOILERPLATE"
EVEN IF I HEARD THAT, I DIDN'T HEAR IT..
SCHULZ

I HAVE BAD NEWS FOR YOU.. I HOPE YOU WON'T FAINT...
© 1986 United Feature Syndicate, Inc.
YOU CAN'T SUE ANYBODY TODAY BECAUSE IT'S NEW YEAR'S EVE, AND THE COURTHOUSE IS CLOSED..
12-31
KLUNK
NOW I HAVE MORE BAD NEWS...
TOMORROW IS NEW YEAR'S DAY SO YOU CAN'T SUE ANYBODY THEN, EITHER!
KLUNK!
SCHULZ

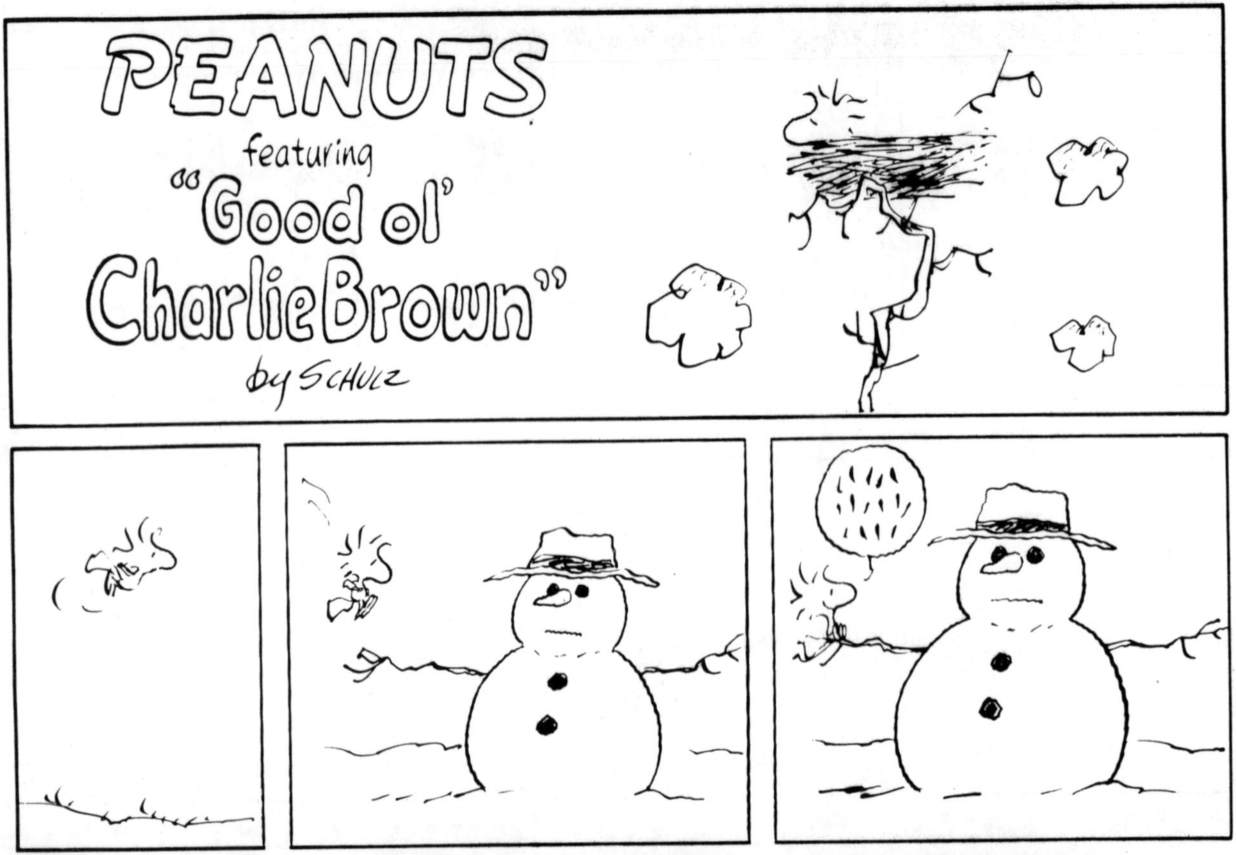
PEANUTS
featuring
"Good ol' Charlie Brown"
by SCHULZ

© 1986 United Feature Syndicate, Inc.
12-21
?
SNOWMEN DON'T HAVE EARS
SCHULZ

1-1-87
YOU'RE GIVING ME A CALENDAR? HOW NICE..
© 1986 United Feature Syndicate, Inc.
I SEE IT HAS PICTURES OF BIRDS ON IT
LET ME GIVE YOU ONE OF MINE..
IT HAS PICTURES OF BEAGLES ON IT!
SCHULZ

YOU THREW AWAY THE CALENDAR I GAVE YOU!
IT HAS PICTURES OF BEAGLES ON EVERY PAGE! BEAGLES JUMPING OVER FENCES! BEAGLES RUNNING ACROSS FIELDS! BEAGLES WINNING "BEST-IN-SHOW"!
1-2-87
HOW COULD YOU DO SUCH A THING?!
HE WANTED TO TRY OUT HIS NEW WASTEBASKET
SCHULZ
© 1986 United Feature Syndicate, Inc.

HEY, MARCIE.. DID YOU FINISH "WAR AND PEACE"? YOU DID?
IT'S AWFULLY LONG, ISN'T IT? I COULDN'T READ THE WHOLE THING
© 1986 United Feature Syndicate, Inc.
NO, I JUST SORT OF SKIPPED THROUGH IT...
1-3-87
This is my report on skipping through "War and Peace"
SCHULZ

YES, MA'AM.. I GUESS IT WAS KIND OF A MESSY PAPER...
© 1986 United Feature Syndicate, Inc.
I'VE TRIED, BUT I CAN'T BE NEAT LIKE MARCIE HERE..
YOU SHOULD SEE HER ROOM AT HOME, MA'AM.. HER CLOSET AND DRESSER DRAWERS ARE SO NEAT...
1-5-87
I THINK SHE KEEPS HER SOCKS IN ALPHABETICAL ORDER!
YOU'RE WEIRD, SIR..
SCHULZ

12-27
AND NOW A TRAFFIC REPORT..
HOLIDAY TRAFFIC IS HEAVY GOING INTO THE CITY..
© 1986 United Feature Syndicate,Inc.
A TRAILER IS OVERTURNED AT THE ENTRANCE TO THE BRIDGE...
NEAR THE CORNER WE HAVE A STALLED SKATEBOARD..
SCHULZ

Dear Grandma and Grandpa,
They say that grandparents like to spoil their grandchildren.
© 1986 United Feature Syndicate,Inc.
1-6-87
I'm ready when you are.
SCHULZ

LISTEN TO THOSE VIOLINS! BOY, I'D LOVE TO PLAY IN AN ORCHESTRA...
YOU COULD DO IT, SIR..
OF COURSE, YOU'D HAVE TO PRACTICE
© 1986 United Feature Syndicate, Inc.
1-7-87
I'D HAVE TO **WHAT**?
SCHULZ

NO, I'VE NEVER RUN WITH THE HOUNDS.. MY DAD DID, THOUGH...
HE SAID HE FELL IN A HOLE, RAN INTO A TREE, WAS STEPPED ON BY A HORSE AND BITTEN BY A FOX!
© 1986 United Feature Syndicate, Inc.
1-8-87
I SAID TO HIM, "THAT MUST HAVE BEEN A LONG DAY.."
HE SAID, "NO, THAT ALL HAPPENED IN THE FIRST FIVE MINUTES!"
SCHULZ

PEANUTS
featuring
"Good ol'
Charlie Brown"
by Schulz

SHOVEL YOUR WALK?

1-4-87

ALL THREE OF YOU?

I DO THE HARD WORK..MY ASSISTANT DOES THE EDGES
© 1986 United Feature Syndicate,Inc.
WHAT DOES THE LITTLE GUY DO?
WHEN WE'RE ALL DONE, HE SWEEPS UP THE SNOW CRUMBS!

HEY! YOU GUYS LOOK GOOD TOGETHER!
I'M IMPRESSED
LET'S SEE ONE OF YOUR LIFTS..
© 1986 United Feature Syndicate, Inc.
1-9-87
THAT MAY NEED A LITTLE WORK..

THERE'S A LOT OF HISTORY IN THE DESERT
ESPECIALLY IN THE ROCKS
SOMETIMES YOU CAN FIND MARKINGS THAT WERE PROBABLY MADE A MILLION YEARS AGO...
© 1986 United Feature Syndicate, Inc.
KILROY WAS HERE
SCHULZ 1-10-87